AMAZING

CONTENTS

AMAZING TRICKS

You can perform some amazing tricks!

Try the experiments in this book and see what happens.

STICKY TRICKS

Sticky Balloon Trick

Blow up a balloon.
Rub the balloon against your head for about 30 seconds.

Hold the balloon so that it's touching a wall.

Let go of the balloon.

What do you notice?

Magnetic Pencil Trick

Hold two pencils
with your fingertips.

Press them together
as hard as you can.

Then, very slowly,
try to pull them apart.

What do you notice?

Magic Comb Trick

Cut a piece of paper
into many small pieces.
Put the pieces into a pile.

Use a medium-sized or large
comb to comb your hair.

Hold the comb a few
centimetres above the pile
of paper.

What do you notice?

AWESOME ARM TRICKS

Automatic Arms Trick

Stand in a doorway with the outside of your hands pressed against the frame. Keep your arms straight. Press hard for 90 seconds.

Step away from the door.

What do you notice?

Did you notice that your arms felt like they were starting to float upwards?

Amazing Shrinking
Arms Trick

Face a wall and stretch out
your arms to touch it.

Now bend your arms
and rub your elbows.

Stretch your arms again.
Try to touch the wall.

What do you notice?

Did you notice that your arms seemed to be shorter the second time?

Shake out your arms. Stretch them a third time. Did your arms seem longer again?

RIGHT BEFORE YOUR EYES

Deceiving Dot Trick

Look at the red dot on this page for about one minute.

Now look hard at
a piece of white paper.

What do you notice?

Did you notice that you saw a
different-coloured dot when you
stared at the white paper?

Old Switcheroo Trick

Draw a small square inside a larger square.

Colour the inside square green. Colour the outside square blue.

Stare at your picture for about one minute. Then close your eyes tight.

What do you notice?

Floating Finger
Sausage Trick

Hold your arms out
in front of your face.
Put your index fingers
together at the fingertips.

Now look hard at your fingers
and slowly bring your fingers
towards your nose.

What do you notice?

Disappearing Hat Trick

Close your left eye. Stare at the star with your right eye.

Hold the picture close to your face. Slowly move the picture away from your face while staring at the star with your right eye.

What do you notice?

21

Bending Spoon Trick

Fill a clear glass $^3/_4$ full of water. Put a spoon inside the glass.

Hold your head so that your eyes are even with the top of the water.

What do you notice?

INDEX